Meet the Twitch...

By Hayley Scott   Illustrated by Pippa Curnick

USBORNE

Chapter One
Moving Day

Stevie Gillespie was precisely 117.5 centimetres tall, with long brown hair that she wore in a big plait on one side of her head. She had it on the side so she could twirl it between her fingers when she was thinking.

Stevie liked:

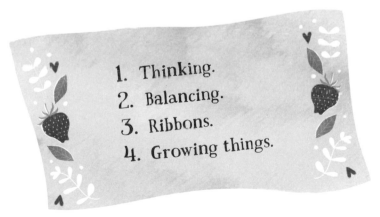

1. Thinking.
2. Balancing.
3. Ribbons.
4. Growing things.

Her favourite food was strawberries. Or those sweets that look like fried eggs. Or mashed potato with lots of ketchup. She had grey eyes, hundreds of freckles and two favourite outfits.

One of them was this:

And the
other one
was this:

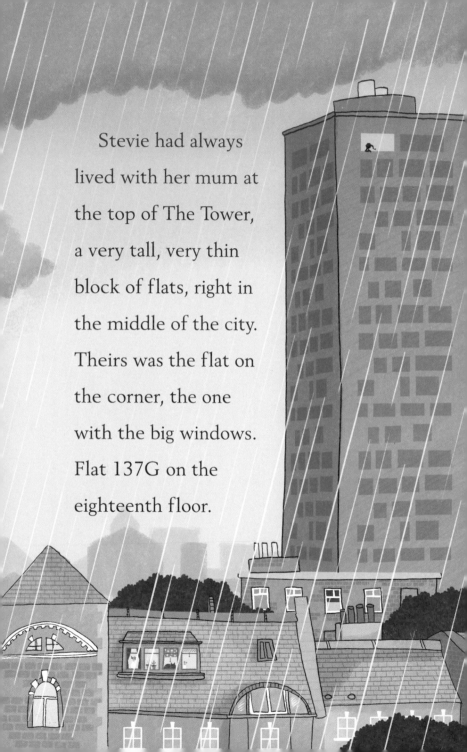

Stevie had always
lived with her mum at
the top of The Tower,
a very tall, very thin
block of flats, right in
the middle of the city.
Theirs was the flat on
the corner, the one
with the big windows.
Flat 137G on the
eighteenth floor.

When it was raining, as it was today, Stevie liked to sit and watch the water splash against the glass, and *think*.

But today was different. Today all their stuff was being taken away in a big truck and Stevie and her mum were moving to a cottage in the countryside *miles* away. Stevie liked her old room, her old school, her old friends and she really, really, *really* didn't want to go.

Mum was crossing off and adding things to her big list. They were nearly ready. Stevie twirled her plait, said nothing, and watched the morning clouds change shape as they

floated across the sky. A row of
fluffy kittens skipped in a line. Their
tails waved high and their paws left a
spatter of cloud footprints behind
them.

If Stevie had her own list it would say:

> ### Good Things About Moving to the Country
> 1. **Live nearer Dad.**
> 2.

Stevie was stuck on number two.

At times like this, Stevie would usually water her plants, and sometimes talk to them, but she couldn't because they'd already been packed and driven off. This was not a good day.

Just then, there was a buzz at the door.

"Get that would you please, love?" said Mum.

Odds & Ends

Stevie dragged her
chair all the way over
to the door so
she could
stand on it and
look through the
little round
spyhole.

There, squashed up and a funny
shape through the glass, was Nanny
Blue, who was holding a big box
wrapped in pale blue paper and tied up
with a shimmery bow.

"Nanny Blue!" Stevie opened the door and dived towards her grandmother, who put the parcel down so she could give Stevie a big squeeze.

"Hello, Stevie!" said Nanny Blue.

Stevie squeezed Nanny Blue really tightly back.

"Let's not beat about the bush," said Nanny Blue, grinning and letting go of Stevie.

She pointed at the parcel. "You'd better open this."

The paper was so shiny it sparkled and the label attached to it said:

To Stevie,
with lots of love from Nanny Blue.

A new house for a new house.
May you have lots of adventures.

x x x

Chapter Two
A Special Gift

Stevie pulled the ribbon gently, then ripped at the paper at top speed. Her heart was beating fast and her fingers trembled.

"Oh!"

Inside the box was a beautiful teacup that was far too big to be filled with tea. Instead, it was topped off with a round, flat roof made from

lots of little blue tiles, which sat
perfectly on the cup's rim.

What could it be? Stevie took a
deep breath and lifted it out.

It was a teacup house! It had
eight windows and a front door
and a back door, and was decorated
with a bright pattern of leaves and
flowers. It had all the details of a real
house too: pipes, guttering, a door
knob, even a little letter box!

There was a saucer, which,
when Stevie sat the teacup in it, she
saw was a wonderful garden with its
very own dainty stone path.

Over the blue door there
was a miniature sign that said:
The Twitches.

Nanny Blue lifted off the roof,
released a tiny catch and swung open
the two halves of the cup, which were

hinged together on one side, so
that Stevie could see inside the
teacup house. It looked like this:

"Oh!" said Stevie. "Thank you!" Her heart was beating even faster.

"You'll need these," said Nanny Blue, reaching into her bag to bring out a shoebox, which had FURNITURE ETC. written in big letters on the side. "But I think you should save them until you're at the cottage."

"It's something to look forward to, right, Stevie?" said Mum.

Nanny Blue and Mum gave each other a secret grown-up look that told Stevie they thought this would make her happy about the move. For once, she didn't care. She was desperate to set up the house and start playing right now. Then she had a thought.

"Where are the dolls?"

Nanny Blue laughed and looked at Mum. "Who said anything about dolls?"

Nanny Blue reached into her bag and brought out a small cotton drawstring bag which she gave to Stevie.

Inside there were four packages, neatly wrapped in blue, starry tissue paper. Stevie took one out. *What could be inside?* she wondered.

When Stevie opened the first package she found a very small, grey toy rabbit.

She had two glittering beads for
eyes, two long ears and a soft velvet
nose. She stood upright like a
person, but had movable arms and
legs, and rabbit paws. There was a

faded paper
label attached
to her dress
with a safety
pin, which
read Silver
Twitch.

Silver Twitch

Stevie removed the label and put it and the safety pin in her pocket.

Stevie placed the rabbit on the garden saucer, where she stood on the grass, perfectly balanced on her big rabbit feet. Her bead eyes shone in the sunlight that came through the window of the flat.

"She's the little girl rabbit," said Nanny Blue.

Then Stevie ripped open the three other packets. Soon, there was a whole family of little rabbits in front of her, each dressed in old-fashioned clothes. She unpinned and pocketed

the other name labels,
and stood them all in
a line in the saucer
garden.

Gabriel, Bo, Silver
and Fig Twitch. A father,
mother, sister and
brother rabbit.

Stevie sensed a funny feeling in the air. Maybe it was the appearance of the tiny rabbits. Maybe it was how the sunlight fell through the windows, so very high up in the sky, shining on all the falling dust. But, for just a moment, everything felt like magic.

"Are you sure you're all right to wait to give the keys to the estate agent?" said Stevie's mum to Nanny Blue, breaking the magic and bringing Stevie back to earth with a harsh bump.

Nanny Blue nodded. "Ring me before bedtime," she said kindly.

"I'll ring you as soon as we get there," said Stevie, popping all four rabbits back into their bag and clutching it firmly between her curled up fingers. She squeezed Nanny Blue as tightly as she possibly could and gave her a really big kiss. Then, she and Mum turned to leave Flat 137G for the very last time.

Chapter Three
A Shock Discovery

When Mum and Stevie finally pulled up into the driveway of their new cottage, Stevie felt a sharp pang in her tummy. The further they'd driven from the city, the worse she'd felt.

"Oh, isn't it pretty, Stevie!" said Mum.

Stevie said nothing. A huge, hot, fat tear rolled down her cheek. She grabbed the bag full of the Twitches and stomped up the path, leaving Mum to follow behind with the boxed teacup house and its furniture.

Stevie's head was full of her *real* home. Flat 137G. She looked up to the sky, but all the clouds were shapes she'd never seen before, just puffed-up blibs and blobs and definitely no kittens.

She felt so sad and so cross that she didn't notice she hadn't pulled the string tight enough to close the top of the Twitches's bag. As she and Mum made their way towards the door of the cottage, neither of them saw one of the rabbits fall out of the bag and into the overgrown grass below.

The door to the cottage was wide open and a man and a woman wearing matching T-shirts that said *We Move You!* were trying to get the grey sofa in through the wooden door frame.

"It's a funny shape, this door, Ms Gillespie," said the man as they wrestled with the sofa.

"We'll get there though, don't you worry," said the woman, smiling. But Stevie wasn't so sure and she just hoped they'd carried her plants safely.

In the kitchen, Mum, who was still holding the teacup house in its box, said, "Who's for a cup of tea or a hot chocolate?" She'd brought a kettle, some teabags, hot chocolate, milk and a packet of biscuits with her in a cardboard box.

"Yes please," said the *We Move You!* people.

"No thank you," said Stevie. "Can I see my room now please?"

Mum took Stevie up the winding staircase, which was wonky and dark and Stevie nearly slipped.

Her new bedroom had:

1. A big window that looked onto the garden.

2. A huge wooden desk.

3. A funny smell.

"You sure you don't want a cup of tea?" said Mum.

Stevie shook her head and reached into her pocket. Out came:

1. A button from her old school uniform.

2. The ribbon from Nanny Blue's parcel.

3. The four safety pins from the Twitches's name labels.

4. A packet of fried-egg sweets.

5. An empty pick 'n' mix bag.

6. Fluff.

Stevie ripped open the sweet packet and shoved all of the eggs into her mouth in one go. As she chewed, she looked Mum straight in the eye, and dropped the wrapper and the rest of the stuff from her pocket onto the desk.

Mum sighed and said nothing. She put the box with the teacup house on the desk and went back downstairs, muttering something as she went.

Stevie reached to open the window for some fresh air – the smell was awful – and put the bag of Twitches on the desk. Then she removed the roof and opened the cup out like Nanny Blue had shown her. It had two floors and each floor had three rooms. Upstairs had a bedroom on one side and another bedroom and a bathroom on the other. Downstairs had a living room to the left, and a kitchen and a study to the right.

There were miniature light switches in each room and when Stevie pressed them, all the lights, which were like old-fashioned gas lamps, came on.

The whole teacup house glowed a faint orange, like a real house in the distance at night-time.

Stevie started opening the shoebox full of furniture. Soon, on the desk in front of her, were:

1. A big disorganized collection of furniture, ready to make the teacup house a very comfortable place indeed.

2. A box of pretend food, full of

bread, fruit, cheese and cake.

3. Lots of Twitch-sized books,
with real pages.

Stevie took the Twitches from
their bag. She placed each rabbit in
the teacup's saucer garden.

Bo.

Silver.

Fig.

Stevie picked up the Twitches's bag. She patted it. She tipped it upside down. She turned it inside out and back again. She reached inside the bag and felt a panic as she realized the fourth Twitch was definitely not there.

Without hesitation, she ran onto the landing, stood at the top of the stairs and shouted as loudly as she could, "Mum! Mum! Come quickly! The daddy Twitch is missing!"

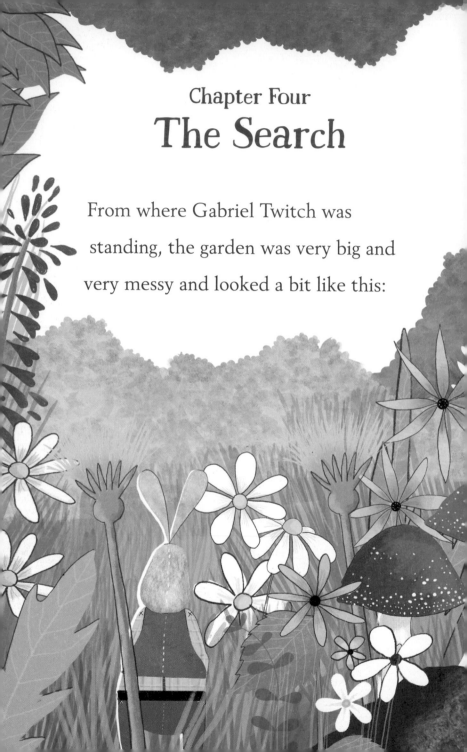

Chapter Four
The Search

From where Gabriel Twitch was standing, the garden was very big and very messy and looked a bit like this:

This much
he knew: he'd
nodded off on
the journey to
the new house.

Then, he'd woken
up with a bump and
an "Ouch!"

He could only guess they'd arrived and that he'd fallen out of the bag somehow, when Stevie and her mum had taken everyone else inside.

He knew one more thing: he needed to get to his family, but from his position in the long grass he really couldn't see how.

Very close to where he stood, growing tall and strong, were six sturdy-looking toadstools. Gabriel decided to climb onto the shortest one to get a better look at his surroundings.

The daddy rabbit pulled himself up
on top of the first toadstool, looked all
about him, and could just see a cottage.
They must be in there!
He had to move fast.
Without thinking,
off he went,

jump...

jump...

bouncing from one
toadstool to the next.

jump...

Then, with one final big

jump,

Gabriel Twitch got himself
into a terrible fix...

He'd jumped too far and
overbalanced, slipping
from the edge of
the very last
toadstool and...

falling,

falling,

until he landed in something that
was like a very gluey, sticky string.

No matter how much he twisted and turned, wriggled and jiggled, squiggled and squirmed, he couldn't get out.

Oh no! What was going on?

It didn't take Gabriel long to realize he'd got himself totally and utterly tangled up in a spiderweb. He'd seen them before, inside, wispy and in faraway corners of humans' rooms. But this was different. This was gungy and wet. And he was stuck in it! What was he to do? He looked about him anxiously and felt frightened to realize there was nothing he could do about it whatsoever…

If only his family inside the

cottage knew where he was.

Silver Twitch opened her eyes and yawned. She was lying on the soft, neat grass lawn of the saucer garden. She stood up, gave a little jump, and shook out her long rabbit ears.

"That's better," she said, as she twitched her nose, sniffing the air to make sure Stevie wasn't there. She began to skip across the garden to find the rest of her family.

"Hello, sweetheart," said Bo Twitch, as her daughter hopped past.

"Hello, Mama!" said Silver.

The
Twitches

Mama Bo straightened her dress. "And where are your brother and your father?" she said, looking about her.

"I'm here," said Silver's little brother Fig, popping up from the back garden. "And I'm starving."

Silver and Mama Bo laughed. "Aren't you always?" said Mama.

Fig was about to put the carrot that was permanently attached to his paw into his mouth. He never learned. "Yuck!" he said spitting out the carrot. "Why didn't someone think to fix some delicious cake to me instead? Not all rabbits like carrots, you know."

"We know," said Mama Bo. "You've mentioned it once or twice." The three rabbits laughed. "Let's find your father, and get some food."

"Gabriel!"
she called.

"Daddy!"
called Silver and Fig.

There was no reply.

"That's strange," said Mama Bo. She had a funny feeling, and it wasn't a good one.

"Gabriel!"

she shouted again.

"Daddy!"

shouted the

other two.

Silver and Fig were starting to get

worried too. This didn't feel right at all.

There was still no reply. The rabbit family looked around them. The teacup house felt unfriendly without all the furniture set up inside it. They walked up and down the stairs and moved from one empty room to another. The untidy pile of their furniture and things on Stevie's desk somehow looked quite threatening.

They hadn't heard Stevie talking about putting their daddy rabbit somewhere else. In the car, before they'd all dozed off, she'd been talking about setting them up straight away, all four of them, in the teacup house.

"You know," said Mama Bo
eventually, pulling the little rabbits
towards her apron, "I think Daddy
Gabriel has got lost."

Chapter Five
Silver's Invention

Stevie ran back into her bedroom, pulling at her mum's sleeve. She pointed at the three Twitches. That was strange. She was sure she'd left them in the saucer garden. But now they were inside the teacup house.

No, she must have imagined it. But she hadn't imagined that there were only three Twitches. Gabriel was still missing.

"Look! He isn't there!" she said desperately.

Mum looked around the room. "He can't have gone far," she said calmly. "You had them out on your lap several times in the car, all four of them, remember? Let's start there and work our way back towards the house. He'll be here somewhere."

Stevie twirled her plait and tried not to cry.

"Thanks, Mum," she said softly.

As soon as Stevie and her mum had

gone, the three rabbits began chattering.

"How do we know Stevie didn't drop your daddy on the floor in *here*?" said Mama Bo sensibly. "He might still be asleep, *down there* somewhere." All three rabbits peered over the edge of Stevie's desk.

It was a *very* long way down.

"Daddy Gabriel!" called the rest
of his family over the edge of the desk.
"Where are you?"

There was no reply.

"Daddy Gabriel!
Just shout if you're
down there!"

There was still no reply.

"At least Stevie is looking for him," said Mama Bo.

"Well, we'll have to look for him too," said Silver decisively. "We can't *leave* him lost, can we?"

"Wait a moment. Can I borrow your binoculars please, Silver?" said Mama Bo.

Silver passed them over. Mama Bo held them up and turned, very slowly, to look at as much of the room around and below her as she possibly could.

"It's no good," she said eventually. "I definitely can't see him down there. Silver's right. We're going to have to go and look for him."

"But how?" asked Fig, nervously.

65

"*You're* not, *I* am," said Silver. "Just give me a moment. I need to think." She knew she couldn't jump. She didn't have a rope, or a ladder. She wished that she had a giant slide to *whoosh* all the way down to the carpet. Gosh, that would be fun! And then she had a thought.

"I saw something in one of my books once. I can't remember what it was called, and if all our stuff wasn't stacked so higgledy-piggledy, I'd dig the book out and find it. But it was a thing that helped people jump safely out of an aeroplane. A thing people wear on their backs that sort of pops out when they jump!" She clapped her paws together excitedly. "I think I could use some of the things Stevie's left on the desk right here, and make one…"

"Make what exactly?" asked Mama Bo and Fig at the same time.

"I'm going to make a… paperfloatyfallingthing!"

Mama Bo and Fig looked at each other uncertainly, but Silver remembered the picture from the book and started picking up things that had been left on the desk.

1. Ribbon.
2. Blue, starry tissue paper.
3. The four safety pins from their name labels.
4. Two crinkled-up sweet wrappers.

While Mama Bo and her brother looked on, Silver started ripping, tying, pinning and looping the bits and pieces together. She pinched and plaited. She squeezed, sheared and snipped.

In almost no time at all she'd made her very own paperfloatyfallingthing.

She even made herself a helmet,
by wrapping a piece of ribbon around
Stevie's old button and tying the
ribbon under her chin.

"Ta-da!" she said proudly.

Fig burst into
applause and
Mama Bo
nodded
slowly.

Over the years she'd seen Silver make all sorts of things. She really was a clever rabbit. Mama wished that she could go with Silver to help, but somebody needed to look after Fig. Besides, what if Daddy Gabriel came back to find the house empty?

"Well…" said Mama Bo.

"I'm all set!" said Silver. Her tummy twisted and jiggled with nerves and excitement and, of course, a gulp of fear.

"You be careful," said Mama Bo.

"Ready…" said Fig, who wished he was old enough to go with his sister. "Steady… GO!"

Silver gripped tightly to the strings of her strange-looking contraption and ran towards the edge of the desk. She slipped, slithering over the edge too quickly, and for a moment she dropped, like she was going to fall instead of float.

She felt the thud-thud of her heart in her chest, and she worried she'd accidentally let go.

Mama Bo and Fig gasped and watched from behind their paws. But then the whole thing opened out and began to float gently – just like a paperfloatyfallingthing!

Down, down, down

Silver floated.
She felt wonderful!

Down,

down,

down...

And then, after the
best feeling she could possibly
imagine, Silver Twitch landed on
the carpet with a perfect, gentle
bump.

"Made it!" she said triumphantly, untying the ribbon of her button helmet and giving the air a little punch. The top of the desk was far, far away now, but she could still see Mama Bo and Fig, clapping furiously at her achievement.

Silver pushed the paperfloaty-fallingthing carefully underneath the desk in case she needed it later. Then she began to work her way across the carpet of Stevie's bedroom, looking

to see if Daddy Gabriel had somehow
fallen into a hole or a corner or a nook.

"Daddy! Daddy! Are you
here?"

"Daddy! Gabriel!"

Fig and Mama Bo peered

over the desk's edge.

There was still no reply.

As Silver searched,

she felt her heart

beat faster with

worry.

She couldn't

see Daddy Gabriel.

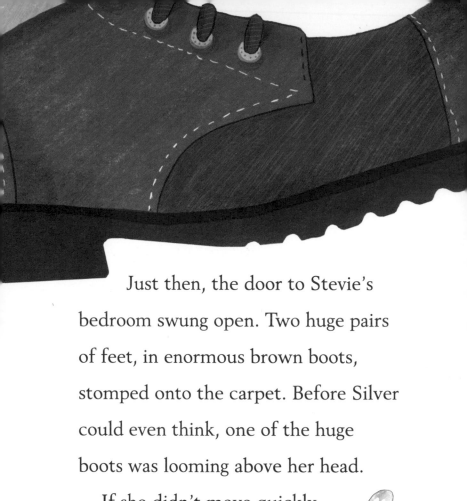

Just then, the door to Stevie's
bedroom swung open. Two huge pairs
of feet, in enormous brown boots,
stomped onto the carpet. Before Silver
could even think, one of the huge
boots was looming above her head.

If she didn't move quickly,
she was going to get totally
squashed!

Chapter Six
A Bumpy Ride

Silver gasped as the giant foot and a big cardboard box crashed down hard next to her on the carpet. She rolled quickly out of the way.

"Oh no!" Silver heard the woman say. "This box says KITCHEN on it. We'll have to take it back downstairs!"

Silver looked around her one more time and called out in a whisper, "Daddy! Daddy! Are you there?" But there was still no answer.

She looked up and saw Mama Bo and Fig standing perfectly still by the edge of the desktop. They couldn't be any help when people were about and Silver had a very clear thought: *Daddy Gabriel must be somewhere out there. The removal people are going out there.*

As both people lifted the large box and made to leave Stevie's bedroom, Silver noticed that one of the man's shoelaces was undone and the wiggly string hung there, right in front of her. The man wouldn't see the lace because he was helping to carry the

big box, which would shield his view of
his feet. Which meant that the man
wouldn't see Silver if she…

Silver grabbed onto the end of
the removal man's shoelace
and clung onto it as tightly
as she could with her tiny
rabbit paws. She looked
up at Mama Bo and

Fig, who were both still frozen in place. Mama Bo was holding her paw over her little mouth in shock. Fig's paw was holding onto his mum's apron. Silver took a deep breath, closed her eyes, and felt herself

bump,

bump,

bump

along the carpet, out of the bedroom and into the unknown…

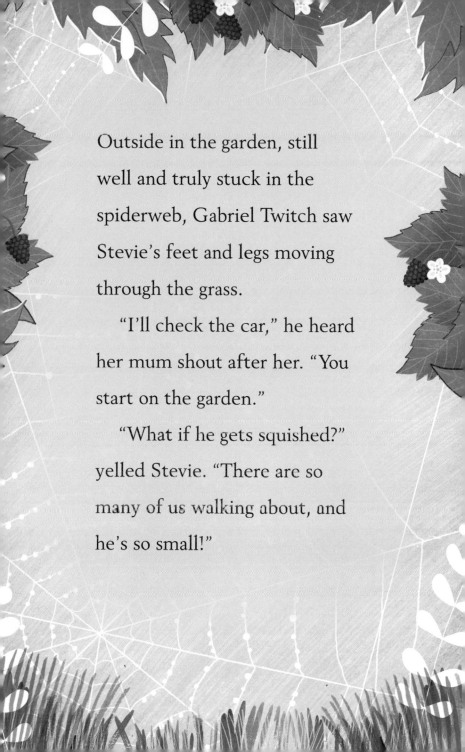

Outside in the garden, still well and truly stuck in the spiderweb, Gabriel Twitch saw Stevie's feet and legs moving through the grass.

"I'll check the car," he heard her mum shout after her. "You start on the garden."

"What if he gets squished?" yelled Stevie. "There are so many of us walking about, and he's so small!"

"Squished! *No!*" Gabriel shouted, but nobody heard him. His voice was too quiet for any human to hear, and he felt helpless as Stevie's legs and feet moved further away from him, to the other end of the garden.

Gabriel saw Stevie drop to her hands and knees and start to work her way through the lawn, looking for him in all the wrong places.

Meanwhile Silver was bouncing and swinging all the way down the staircase of the cottage, holding tightly to the shoelace.

"Ouch... oomph... oooh... ouch!"

It really was an uncomfortable ride!
She hoped that as long as she held
on she'd be fine.

Bump,

bump,

bump,

"Ouch!"

All around her the patterns of the
carpet swirled and whirled, and she felt
more dizzy with each giant step.

When the removal people finally got
to the bottom of the stairs they stopped,
and the shoelace flicked back with one
last big **thwack!**

Silver wasn't going to risk getting
crushed by the massive box, or by
any gigantic feet, so she immediately
let go, flying through the air like
she'd been launched by a very strong
catapult.

She flew,

and flew,

then rolled, rolled, rolled, all along the skirting board, all along the edge of the kitchen floor, all the way to the frame of the front door, where she stopped with a big **thump**.

While the big feet stomped about behind her, and there was the sound of boxes being dragged and unstacked, Silver crouched, out of view, by the door. She couldn't believe her eyes. She'd never seen *anything* like this.

There before her was a big sky, and a giant-sized garden. Flowers as tall as towers, and thick shocks of grass that were dotted with dandelions and daisies. It was very pretty, very scary, and very new. And somewhere out there was Daddy Gabriel.

How on earth was she going to find him?

Chapter Seven
In the Garden

Silver hopped off the step and made
her way along the edge of the path.
She scampered towards the tall grass,
making sure to keep hidden as much
as she could behind plant pots on the
paving stones. The sky was so bright
and the air felt cold on her little
rabbit cheeks. She could smell
the flowers and the strangeness
of everything. She gulped.
She could do this.

The grass was long and thick in front of her, but Silver wasn't going to give up now, not when she'd come so far. She leaned against the stalk of a nearby dandelion and took a deep breath. She'd never even been outside before! "Daddy!" she called in her loudest voice. "Daddy! Are you here?"

She waited and watched the removal man and woman stomp back across the garden towards their truck to get more things. *Please don't squish him*, she thought. *Please don't squish him.* Their feet were so big and she'd nearly been squished herself!

"Daddy!" she shouted once again. "Daddy!"

But there was no reply. Or was there? Silver thought she had heard a familiar voice, tiny, ever so quiet, from far away.

"Silver! Silver! Is that you?"

Silver began to run as fast as she could towards the voice. "Daddy! I'm coming! It's me!"

She ran and hopped and swished through the looming grass.

Flowers bobbed and brushed against her, trying to block the way, but she didn't stop. She just ran and hopped, ran and hopped, as fast as she could.

And then, among a patch of bobbing
dandelions, Silver Twitch came face-to-
face with eight long, hairy legs, eight beady
eyes, and two big, spiky fangs. It was a
monster! Silver gave out a little scream,
rubbed her eyes to be sure – and realized
she was, in fact, looking at a giant spider!

It really was the most terrifying thing she'd ever seen. A spider that was as big as she was!

Silver stood very still.

The spider stood very still.

Who was going to move first?

Silver was as still as she could be.

The spider took one, two, three
steps towards her. Silver didn't move.
Four steps, five, six, seven…eight.
Silver saw the reflection of
her face in the eight shiny eyes
as they moved nearer.

The hairs on the creature's hideous legs were so close now they began to tickle her fur, and for one awful moment she thought she might sneeze. She took a really deep breath, but her nose tingled, and her eyes watered. She wasn't sure if she could stop herself!

Suddenly, there was a rustle in the dandelions behind them. Something was moving in the bushes. Quick as a flash, the spider turned away and scurried into the undergrowth.

Silver let out a big, very relieved sigh. "Phew! That was close!"

And then, just as Silver was deciding

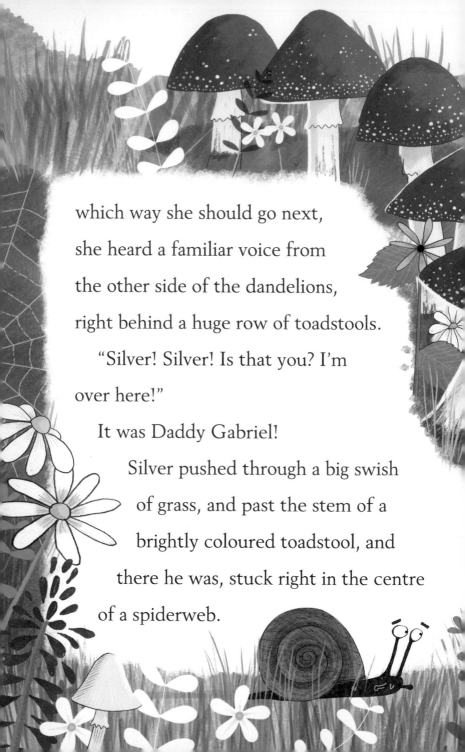

which way she should go next,
she heard a familiar voice from
the other side of the dandelions,
right behind a huge row of toadstools.

"Silver! Silver! Is that you? I'm
over here!"

It was Daddy Gabriel!

Silver pushed through a big swish
of grass, and past the stem of a
brightly coloured toadstool, and
there he was, stuck right in the centre
of a spiderweb.

He really was in a mess, all covered in gluey thread, and totally unable to move. But it was most definitely Daddy Gabriel.

For a moment, Silver watched him bounce and sway in the breeze with shock, which soon became delight. She'd never felt so happy in her life, although she knew she'd have to get him out of the web, of course!

"I've come to rescue you!" she said proudly.

"You really have!" said Daddy Gabriel.

Looking about her, Silver spotted a strong-looking dandelion, and pulled as

hard as she could, pushing away the
leaves to get to the root. *Heave! Heave!*
It really was hard work, but she didn't
give up and, finally, out it came, with
one last heave. Soon Silver was using the
stalk to tear
at the web,
chopping
and swiping
into the grey
threads until they
fell in thick, sticky
pieces onto the
ground. Daddy
Gabriel was free!

Silver gave him the biggest cuddle,
and he gave her a kiss on top of her
head, in between her
floppy ears.

"What now?" he
asked, brushing the

last of the web from his collar.

"Hmmm…" Silver looked around them. She remembered Stevie opening her bedroom window earlier, when they'd first arrived. She looked up at the cottage and saw that creeping ivy grew all the way up its wall. And the window was still slightly open. "We're going to climb," she said.

The path from where they stood
   to the house wasn't long,
      but they'd be out in the open,
      so they'd have to be careful.

Silver and Daddy Gabriel crept through the grass, keeping to the shadows. As they got closer, the wall loomed before them like a ginormous mountain.

Stevie and Mum came back to the front door, just as Silver and Gabriel reached the bottom of the ivy. Their shadows covered the rabbits in a spooky darkness.

"We can do this, Daddy," said Silver.

"I hope so," he said, and they squeezed each other's paws for luck.

At the bottom of the ivy the two Twitches, careful but a bit wobbly with

fear, began to climb, up,
up, up, perfectly hidden
amongst the clusters
of bright green
leaves.

Stevie and Mum
were standing right
by them, but they
didn't see a thing.

"He definitely
wasn't in the car,
love," said
Mum.

"I've been looking for ages," Stevie said. "The garden's too big. He could be anywhere!"

"Let's not give up," said Mum. "We'll find him."

"It doesn't help with them stomping all over the place," said Stevie, nodding towards the removal truck. "None of this would have happened if we'd stayed in the city."

"Let's take a break," said Mum. "How about some hot chocolate and a biscuit?"

"But I need to find the daddy
Twitch," said Stevie urgently, twirling
her plait. But she was hungry and her
knees ached from crawling in the grass.
Maybe it wouldn't hurt to stop for a
little while. Then she shook her head.
"I can't believe I've lost him."

"When I was a little girl," said Mum,
leading Stevie into the cottage and
taking two biscuits from the packet
on the kitchen counter, "those rabbits
had a habit of turning up in the most
unlikely places."

"What do you mean?"

"Why don't we take another look in your bedroom?" Mum said. "We didn't really look properly in there. It's been a very tiring day."

Stevie looked at her mum, grabbed her hand, and dragged her towards the stairs immediately.

Chapter Eight
Home at Last

Silver and Daddy Gabriel climbed
head first through the open window.
They both looked dishevelled, with
the odd bit of leaf sticking out of their
clothes and mud on their paws.

But they'd made it – they were
home!

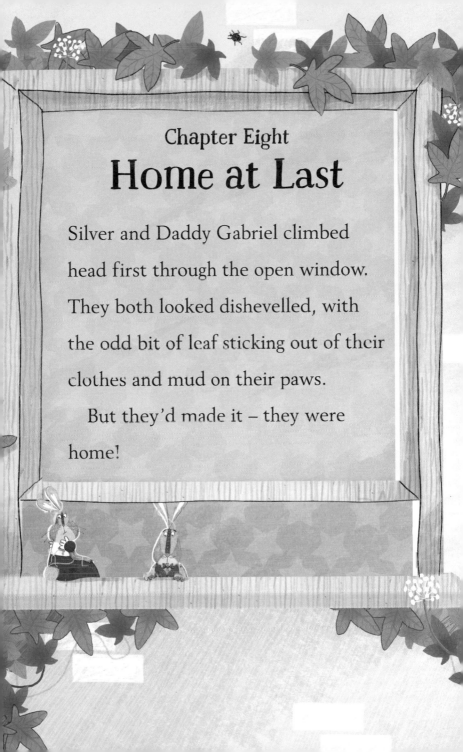

And they slid down the window frame, and jumped onto the desk with a little twirl to prove it!

"It's you!" said all of the Twitches at once. Mama Bo, Fig, Daddy Gabriel and Silver all rushed towards each other, thudding their feet on the desk, rubbing noses and giving each other the biggest, most welcome of hugs.

"However did you do it?" asked Fig excitedly.

"I knew you would," said Mama Bo before anyone could answer. She rubbed her cheek against Daddy Gabriel's, and then against Silver's too.

She was so happy to see them!

"We'll tell you *all* about it later," said Daddy Gabriel, giving Mama Bo a big kiss. "But quick!" They brushed the mud from their clothes just as the handle to Stevie's room turned.

The four Twitches stood perfectly still in the saucer garden of the teacup house.

Stevie, closely followed by Mum, ran over to her desk and counted the toy rabbits.

One, two, three…four.

One. Two. Three. Four.

It couldn't be. It just couldn't.

But there he was, his belt buckle shining, and his little moustache right where it should be. Gabriel Twitch.

"How did you…?" Stevie held him
tight in her hand and looked at him
very carefully. Mum had been right.
But… "I'm sure you weren't here. I'm
sure!" How could she have thought he
was lost when he was right there all
along? Could she *really* have missed
him? "Look, Silver! Fig! It's
your daddy!"

She scooped up
all four
Twitches
and put
them down
inside the

teacup house. "Look! It's your house! Exactly as you left it. Tomorrow you'll have to help me set it all up. We'll have such fun. Maybe you could help me set up my bedroom too…" She looked

around at the boxes of her things.
There was so much to unpack. She'd
have to set everything up just right.

Very carefully, Stevie picked the
little double bed from the stack of the
Twitches's tiny furniture and placed it

neatly inside Mama Bo and Daddy
Gabriel's bedroom. Next, she placed
each Twitch gently in the bed and
covered them with as many blankets
as she could find among their things,
and blew them a kiss goodnight. She
turned off the little lights, and
closed the two sides
of the teacup
house together,

so it sat comfortably in its saucer.

"Night night, Twitches," she said, and tapped the little sign above their door with her finger, so it swung back and forth.

"Thank you, Nanny Blue," she said, smiling her biggest smile.

Tomorrow she would get to play with them at last.

As she made her way to the bedroom door, Stevie nearly slipped on something on the carpet. Leaning down, she found a peculiar thing: a jumble of tissue paper, sweet packets, safety pins and ribbon. They had all got stuck together somehow, and when she held them up in front of her they looked very much like a…a tiny parachute!

No. That was *impossible*. It was just a pile of stuff she'd had in her pocket.

But when she peered at it she was sure it was some kind of design. The ribbons were very evenly spaced apart. And somehow the pins had attached themselves to the other bits and pieces...

Stevie looked back at the teacup house, then at her mum who was still standing at the bedroom door. Stevie thought of the Twitches, tucked up in their bed. Somehow, she felt there was magic in the air.

Inside the teacup house, Daddy Gabriel, Mama Bo and Fig had all fallen fast asleep, squashed together in the bed, each one dreaming about what would happen tomorrow. It had been a busy day!

But Silver was still awake. She was thinking about what it felt like to float through the air, and face the spider, and save Daddy from the web, and... She felt excited. She knew she was ready for another adventure...

Out in the garden, two stripy mugs of hot chocolate sat steaming on the table as Stevie and Mum hung lights on the apple tree, and put coloured lanterns

with bright bulbs in the garden.
They were beautiful in the early
evening light, like candles on a
giant birthday cake.

The garden and the cottage did look lovely, thought Stevie. The lights, the trees, the ivy growing up the side of the house, right up and around the upstairs windows. It wasn't Flat 137G. But it had potential.

"That big plot of earth there," said Mum, nodding to the side of the garden. "That whole space going all the way along the house? You can choose all the plants there – that's just for *you*, Stevie."

Stevie looked at the massive stretch of soil and for a brief moment imagined all the plants, vegetables and

flowers she might grow there. She
imagined huge bursts of leaves and
colour and the smell of lavender.
She imagined her muddy gloves and
wellies, and the extra rows of tiny plants
she'd grow especially to put in little plant
pots in the garden of the teacup house.

Stevie looked up and
twirled her plait. She watched
the early evening clouds.

A row of fluffy kittens
floated across the sky. They
skipped in a line, tails high,
as their paws left a spatter of
cloud footprints behind them.

She saw some other things
too. A unicorn carrying the last
of the sun on
its back.

A floating
balloon.

A dragon.

It *almost* felt like home.

Stevie smiled at Mum and Mum
smiled at Stevie. She was already
wondering what adventures all *four*
Twitches and tomorrow would bring.

Meet the Author

When Hayley Scott was little, she used to make tiny furniture for fairy houses, placing it in scooped out hollows in her back garden. Today, Hayley lives in Norfolk and still loves tiny things. *Teacup House* is her debut series for young readers.

Meet the Illustrator

Pippa Curnick is an illustrator, designer, bookworm and bunny owner. She gets her inspiration from walking in the woods in Derbyshire, where she lives with her partner and their son.

Look out for more Teacup House adventures, coming soon from Hayley and Pippa!

For Nell, with love,
and for making every
day an adventure. (Hayley)

To my Big Sis, Tif,
with tonnes of love. (Pippa)

First published in the UK in 2018 by Usborne Publishing Ltd., Usborne House, 83-85 Saffron Hill, London EC1N 8RT, England. www.usborne.com

Text copyright © Hayley Scott, 2018
The right of Hayley Scott to be identified as the author of this work has been asserted by her in accordance with the Copyright, Designs and Patents Act, 1988.

Illustrations copyright © Usborne Publishing Ltd., 2018
Illustrations by Pippa Curnick.

The name Usborne and the devices ♀♀ are Trade Marks of Usborne Publishing Ltd.

A CIP catalogue record for this book is available from the British Library.

JFMAMJJASO D/17

ISBN 9781474928120 04365/1
Printed in China.